PRESTO

Charles Rammelkamp

BAMBOO DART PRESS

LOS ANGELES † NEW YORK † LONDON † MELBOURNE

Presto by Charles Rammelkamp

ISBN: 978-1-947240-78-0   Paperback

ISBN: 978-1-947240-79-7   eBook

First Printing 2023

Cover art by Dennis Callaci

Layout and design by Mark Givens

For information:

Bamboo Dart Press

chapbooks@bamboodartpress.com

Bamboo Dart Press 037

www.pelekinesis.com

www.bamboodartpress.com

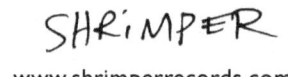

www.shrimperrecords.com

To Abby

Contents

Introduction 6

Information Technology 9

Hell Is Other People 11

Guarded 14

Turf War 16

Painted Into a Corner 18

Profiling 20

Duplicity 22

We Can Be Heroes 24

Driver 27

Reality 29

Extra 32

Survey 35

The Perfect Storm 38

Bartender 41

Primary 44

Dignity for Hire 48

Go to Hell 50

How Sam Spade Got Me Hired and then Fired . . . 53

Stuck 56

Taxi Driver 60

The Same River Twice 62

Mother's Little Helper 65

Acknowledgments 69

Introduction

It's always struck me how much our jobs are our identities. "What do you do?" is often the first question a stranger will ask in a get-acquainted conversation. When I retired at the age of 62, people would often ask me, "What do you do now?" It was as if you didn't exist in space and time without a job. What did I *do*. Indeed, at my retirement party, the card everybody signed said something about "a well-deserved rest."

The story goes that William Burroughs had just one job in his life, as an exterminator, about which he wrote a novel. His various artistic and scholarly endeavors evidently weren't considered "work."

At one point when I'd been out of the job market for longer than my resume could cover, like some sort of alibi ("What were you doing from last May until after Christmas? Why weren't you employed somewhere?"), I signed up to become a Kelly Girl. Maybe they'd already dropped the "girl" at that point and were known instead as Kelly Services. Some of the assignments lasted only a day, stuffing envelopes or doing inventory work in a warehouse; others, in university offices, lasted several weeks. For the longer-term jobs, I sometimes felt as if I were being auditioned, *groomed*, a model going down the runway, an actor reciting lines. Maybe I'd become part of the cast. Wasn't that the aspiration? When was I going to get a *real* job? It's what we all wanted, right? A real job. An identity. To exist.

The adjunct college professor is a special kind of temp worker on the modern college campus: semester-to-semester, slave wages, no benefits, not much in the way of collegial give-and-take. How well I remember coming to the deserted community college after my day job, entering the vacant building, switching on the overhead fluorescent lights, as if in a horror movie, expecting blood and gore on the walls, only to light up the blackboard, the uncomfortable steel-and-wood student desks on the tiled floor. A few minutes later the students would file in like prisoners from a yard break. Then came the business of education.

The idea of a temp worker as a sort of existential hero captured my imagination, a guy making his way through life in the here and now, a sort of "Have Gun Will Travel" dude with a ballpoint pen instead of a derringer. Loyal to nobody, having renounced "membership," an exile on Main Street. A bodhisattva of the workforce.

So I hope the reader identifies with the characters here. By the way, what do *you* do?

Information Technology

"Two all-beef patties?" the man responded, bemused. "Yeah, a Big Mac. What's that for?"

He meant the question, but I ignored him, checked the box on the form on the clipboard I carried.

This is what census-takers must feel like. But I worked for a temp agency (Presto; I was a Presto! It always made me smile when people asked me what I did and I said Presto.) I'd been assigned to do a survey in advance of the release of an animated film about Jesus, or maybe it was Moses, that was being released around Christmas, another five months from now.

"Okay. Did you know that 'Thou shalt not kill' is one of the Ten Commandments?"

"No shit," the guy marveled. News to him. "No, I didn't know that. What's that got to do with McDonald's?"

I checked the box and shrugged slightly.

Ten dollars an hour. This assignment would last most of a week, and then I'd move on, like some sort of Lone Ranger figure. I liked these temporary gigs. You can tolerate anything for a little while, if you're being paid for it. I didn't have a boss leaning over my shoulder. I didn't even have to shave if I didn't want to, but I had anyway.

I'd already checked this guy's responses for "some college," "30 – 40 age range," "$60,000 - $75,000 salary range." There was no box for polo shirt, chinos, or running shoes, but he did say his field was "Information Technology," and I had him pegged for a computer programmer.

"Presbyterian," he answered my next question, "but I don't really belong to any church."

Hell Is Other People

"If they like you, this gig could last indefinitely," Marge told me when I got my new Presto assignment at the Business School. I'd called in to headquarters to check if there was a job; I hadn't worked in about a week. *If they like you. If you're lucky.*

"Thanks, Marge," I mumbled, and the next day I went to the B School.

The job? Filling orders for case study booklets at the university. Various business schools around the country requested copies of relevant case studies for their classes. Titles like *Mobilizing Capital for Development* or *Reshaping the Financial Services Landscape* or *Modern Recruiting: Igniting Organizational Transformation.* IPOs, Paypal, tech-savvy millennials, hedge funds, personnel management. The whole thing made me want to puke, it sounded so deadeningly boring.

"Do you want to be a hired hand all your life?" my mother asked me when I called Sunday. I called her weekly at her home across the country in Potawatomi Rapids, Michigan.

"I don't want to be part of some organization and have bosses and be a boss."

"What's so bad about that?"

"Hell is other people, Mom."

"You can philosophy this all you want, Monsieur Sartre, but facts are facts, situations are situations."

"Exactly."

****

It was Friday and Sid, a regular employee but something of an outsider, was all got up in his partying outfit. He was a guy about my age, maybe a little older, I judged, mid-thirties. He had his hair all slicked up and silver crosses dangling from his ears, otherwise all in black. Sid had a disgusting habit of picking his nose and eating it, not particularly hiding it.

Babs, the supervisor, a Southern Baptist with a twang, rolled her eyes at him, went outside with Conrad for a smoke. Conrad was another temp, like me, though he worked for a different agency.

"You think they're having an affair? Sid asked.

"Are you kidding?" I was going through the stacks gathering copies of a case study called *Leadership in Crisis*. Some school in Arizona needed copies for a class in Entrepreneurship. But then I thought. "They are kind of thick, aren't they?"

"Smoking buddies. Babs doesn't like me, that's for sure."

"Babs. Well." I shrugged. No loss.

The door blew open then on a smell of cigarettes and in came Babs and Conrad. Conrad looked a little old to be a temp, to me, but what was too old, and was I just internalizing my mother's opinions? A bent old guy in his fifties, I judged, with a grizzly goatee. He was always sideling up to sexless Babs.

"Did you get those case studies?" Conrad barked at me, as if he were the boss.

"Don't worry about it."

"Did you?"

I looked at Babs, who looked away. Sid raised his eyebrows. And I saw how it was. Probably angling for a permanent job, Conrad had decided to assume the role of deputy sheriff to Babs' Marshal Dillon. Assistant to the trail boss. And that's how it was done, by taking smoke breaks together. What was in it for Conrad? Did he really think they'd hire him full time? He smelled of desperation. Well, I'd be out of here in a week or two, a month tops.

Guarded

"I don't have to carry a gun, do I?"

"Oh, no, no!" Marge assured, her voice, over the phone, like some bird of prey, shrill and vaguely threatening. "It's just to deter shoplifters, really."

I'd called my Presto supervisor for another assignment. The envelope-stuffing gig at the insurance company had gone three days and I'd been idle for a few days. Now, a department store needed temporary security to handle the holiday consumer binge.

"How do they know I wouldn't shoplift, myself? The fox guarding the henhouse."

"Would you?"

"Well, no, of course not, but how would they know? You'd think they'd do a background check or something, at least."

"That's what we're for. They have our guarantee. Just show up at nine tomorrow. Ask for Megan Martin."

****

"You're here from the temp agency for the security detail? Great. Here, just put on this uniform and come to the conference room to go over your duties with the other temporary security staff. There's coffee and donuts. Help yourself." The lady in the charcoal gray pinstripe pantsuit handed me a jacket, trousers, tie and cap. She had a nameplate on her shoulder that said "Megan."

"Nobody said anything about a uniform."

"You have a problem with that? How else are shoppers supposed to identify you?"

I decided not to argue, knowing it would be futile and I'd just come off as churlish, not a "team player."

"No, I understand," I said, "but I'm really not feeling that well. I shouldn't have come. I think I'd better go home. I'm feeling like I might throw up."

Megan knew I was lying, but, like me, figured there was no point in arguing.

"Okay, well, I'm sorry to hear that. Hope you feel better soon."

"Can I still get a cup of coffee?"

Turf War

"Hey, this is my territory, buddy," the guy in the watch-cap with the three-day stubble growled. It was only my first day of a week-long temp assignment as a pretzel-bike vendor; he might have had a point, I guess, but I was here first and I never thought of street vendors or food trucks as staking a property claim. The whole idea was to be mobile, right?

True, I'd seen guys with the HOMELESS AND HUNGRY signs arguing over choice intersections or expressway exit ramps, but that was more like the law of the jungle at work. I hadn't necessarily been "assigned" the art museum, but Marge, my Presto supervisor, had mentioned it as a likely place to park my bike and sell pretzels. She said the owner had recommended it.

I shrugged, as if to say, sorry, sir, but I wasn't about to leave.

"You hear me, numb nuts? I said this is my beat. So beat it."

"Look, asshole," I replied, taking a similar tough tone. You don't negotiate with bullies. "This is where I was sent. I got here first. Either you can stay and split the business or find someplace else."

"You don't seem to understand," the guy snarled. "I been coming here for a month now, maybe longer."

"A month and you think you own this real estate? Fuck off."

""Prick," Watchcap guy muttered before pedaling off a ways. "You better watch your ass."

There was a big Impressionist show going on at the museum – Renoir, Pissarro, Monet, Cézanne – and a steady stream of people came and went. I did a brisk business in warm, soft pretzels – regular plain salty braided pretzels with a squirt of mustard, avocado ranch sauce, cinnamon sugar, cheddar cheese. It was a breezy spring day, and everybody seemed to want something warm; I kept my own hands warm near the oven. Within four hours I'd sold everything I had. Even made a few dollars in tips.

As I kicked the stand to go back to the garage, the Watchcap dude rode slowly by. He had two of his buddies with him. Silent guys. Muscle.

"How'd it go, asshole?" he asked.

"Sold out. How about you?"

"Lucky for you there's a lot of people here today."

"Yeah, lucky for me," I agreed with an edge of sarcasm, and I pushed off into traffic.

Next day, I decided to go down to the harbor area for a change of scenery. You can find tourists anywhere. Assholes, too, but I didn't need this one in my life.

Painted Into a Corner

"A paint crew? But I've never painted before. What do you mean, how hard can it be? Jesus, Marge. Okay, well. How old are these people I'll be working with? Are we talking about college kids? High school, really? But I don't want to be the older guy who tells them what to do. I mean, I don't even know how to – well, sure, some bookcases, a few walls, but honestly, I'm not, I don't – I mean, I live very modestly, minimum effort. It's not laziness, it's not anything deliberate – sure, maybe a little cheap, but only because that became like a reflex, living frugally, watching expenses. Kind of a monk's ideal. No possessions. But yeah, some day, sure, I'd like to have a family, kids, a house, a mortgage.

"But Geez, a paint crew? I don't know. I've ruined more than one pair of pants doing shit like that. No, I don't have any 'old clothes.' I pretty much wear things until they fall off of me. I stopped growing years ago and don't seem to gain or lose much weight, so the stuff I bought in college still fits fine. The collars of some of my shirts look like they've gone through a paper shredder, and, I don't know, there are holes, but I'm fine with clothing....

"So anyway, if only for the sake of my wardrobe, this paint crew thing could be chancy. Unless they provide paint pants? Smocks? Do you know? Could you find out? I'm not promising anything.

"I know, I know, you aren't doing this as a favor to me,

but if I do a shitty job it isn't going to make you look good either, is it? But I can't guarantee it, Marge, that's the thing. I'm just warning you, it could be more trouble than it's worth.

"No, I don't *think* so. I just mean it *could* be more trouble than it's worth, but, OK, sure. Really, how hard can it be? No, no I should thank *you*, Marge, not the other way around...."

Profiling

"Do you have any ID? Can I see your identification, please?"

"I'm just distributing these flyers for this new pizzeria." I looked at the stack of papers I'd been given. "Luigi's, over on Thirty-sixth Street. It's in that place where Angelo's used to be."

"But do you have any ID? Can you show me some ID?"

"It's just an assignment from the temp agency I work for. I'm a Presto." I smiled, aiming for "unthreatening," even "friendly," but this guy apparently took it as snide, my smile a smirk.

"Don't get smart with me," he snarled, a retiree from the looks of him, white guy in his sixties, gray hair, a two day stubble, t-shirt. "You're casing the neighborhood, aren't you? Trying to see which houses you can break into, what loose things on the porches you can steal. I know what you're up to. You'd just better move on if you know what's good for you."

There was no way to appease this guy. I shrugged, turned to go.

"I'm calling the police."

I resisted the urge to make a "smart" comeback and went to the next house, left a flyer in the door.

"I know what you look like! I'm warning the neighbors!"

When the police car cruised by fifteen minutes later, I was glad that at least I wasn't black.

Duplicity

"Hello? I'm just calling to thank you for being a supporter of the Homeless Veterans with PTSD Initiative. Your support has really been appreciated over the years.

"Are you sure? Our records show you've made generous contributions to HVPI in the past. We were wondering if we could count on your continued...

"Hello? Hello?"

The supervisor gives me the stink eye. Brandi. She's a leather-skinned Floridian with spiky blond hair and crow's feet around the eyes. In a different time she'd be a pack-a-day smoker.

"Another hang-up? You've got to make them think they *know* you. Say their name, like, 'Hello, Karen? It's Jake McGillicuddy.' Or whatever name you're going by. I wouldn't use your real name. Make them *like* you."

At another phone station, the lady who calls herself Mary O'Brien is brow-beating another potential donor, closing the deal.

"They served this country for you. They're the reason you're able to enjoy your freedom. Now it's our turn to –"

She's a full-timer; started out as a temp, like me, but she was so persuasive they offered her a position in no time. She's a housewife, a mother with children, so these four-hour shifts are perfect for her to make a little bit of money while the kiddies are in school.

It's commission versus an hourly rate here, but if after a while you're not making more than the hourly rate in commissions, they let you loose. It's only a Presto temp gig for me, so I don't mind. I'm already looking forward to this one being over.

I dial another number from my list.

"Hello, Mrs. Connolly? Jasper McFarland here. How are you doing? Listen, I'm calling on behalf of the Homeless Veterans with PTSD. Hello? Mrs. Connolly? Hello? Are you still there?"

Brandi the supervisor shakes her head and moves on to "Mary O'Brien." I wish I didn't disappoint her. But this just isn't who I am.

We Can Be Heroes

"You're joking, right? Yes, you're right, I *do* have a CPR certificate from the Red Cross, but I really don't think I could save anyone from drowning. What are the chances? Good question, Marge, what *are* the chances?

"OK, OK, I'll do it. I can't be picky, right? So, where is it? The Town and Country Swim Club? And to be clear, it's just for one day, right?"

My supervisor proceeds to recite the relevant details.

****

As a Presto, I often feel like a fraud. Goes with the territory. Jack of all trades, master of none. The outsider. But when it comes to filing or typing or proofreading or sales – well, ringing up a cash register – I can get away with it. Nothing too serious at stake. But a lifeguard? True, it's a bit of a hyperbolic title, but there's a crumb of truth there, at least. A *life* guard. One who guards lives.

Thank goodness nobody under the age of eighteen is allowed in the pool area. No wading section where a toddler might go missing until he or she is spotted lying on the bottom of the pool.

I'm not even sure why I took the CPR course in the first place. It was free, and it seemed like good training to have, just in case. But I certainly never had any intentions of trying to resuscitate a complete stranger who's collapsed on the street. You can't just walk away once you've started the compressions and the mouth-to-mouth business, you know. That person is legally your responsibility until the EMTs arrive and take over. I shudder to think of vomit trickling out of the corner of some guy's mouth as I try to revive him. *Save his life.*

Lifesaver, lifeguard.

But I *do* feel like a fraud perched up here on this throne by the side of the pool, surveying the lanes of the swimmers doing their laps, back and forth, back and forth.

To be clear, I have no idea how to measure the proper chlorine levels or regulate the water temperature, and the club manager knows this. She says they can get by for one day until the regular lifeguard returns. Some sort of emergency at home, I gather, and the back-up is out of town. All I have to do is – guard lives.

I don't even *look* like anybody's idea of a lifeguard (though who ever does?) – tall and muscular, vigilant.

OK, OK, I know the chances are slim I'll be called upon to do much of anything besides retrieve abandoned kickboards and place them in their racks, maintain a stack of dry towels for the club members.

Still...I am exhausted when the day comes to an end, a rubber life raft with air leaked out, though having done nothing more than sit on my throne watching swimmers go back and forth, back and forth, I've been forced to really consider my identity as defined by work. Isn't that, after all, how we're ultimately sized up? The doctor, the lawyer, the college professor, the government official? The brick layer, the computer programmer, the janitor, the businessman, the bum? What you do is what you are.

Heroic of me, maybe, to have done this for one day, but no, I am *not* a lifeguard in any sense of the word. I am ... a Presto.

Driver

"Cashier, driver, gardener, HVAC tech assistant, nursing home aide, sales, warehouse," Marge read to me over the phone. Alphabetically. My fate from A to Z.

"Nursing home," I asked, plucking a position out of the flow of words, as if a bit of flotsam from a stream. "Bedpans, assistance with shots and pills, helping them to the dining hall at mealtimes?"

"Duties as assigned," Marge read again. "You don't need a medical background."

"I wouldn't think so."

"Why not the driver job? I think that would suit you."

I liked that Marge seemed to see me as an individual, with an individual's personal goals, aptitude, preferences. Not just an assembly line Presto.

"What's it involve?"

"An old guy named Foster. He wants a driver to take him to his appointments, dates. He has a car, just needs somebody to drive him."

****

Foster was ancient, shrunken with age, barely able to see over the dashboard, and maybe his eyesight wasn't up to it anyway. He wore a necklace made of human teeth and had a shrunken human skull dangling from the rearview mirror. He sat up front in the passenger's seat, no being chauffeured around for him.

"Wards off the evil eye," he said, when he saw me eyeballing the necklace. I only shrugged.

"Where to?"

"My eye doctor on Albemarle. You know Doctor Wilson? That's OK. I'll show you where."

I looked out the driver's window to check if traffic was clear and then pulled out into the street. I was wearing jeans and button-down shirt but in my mind I was wearing livery, a little bop cap on my head.

"You're a student?" Foster asked after a while, staring straight ahead out the window so I had this weird sensation he was a priest in a confessional, or a shrink.

"No." I felt an impulse to explain myself but didn't know where to begin.

"Left at the light. So you're doing this because you want to?"

"Doing what?"

"Driving."

"I'm a Presto. I do temp jobs. Kind of like a knight errant from days of old. I go from place to place."

Foster chuckled. "A discoverer. An explorer," he mused after a moment. "Start looking for a place to park, Señor Conquistador. We're almost there."

Reality

"Who has the envies?" Gloria called, a thin woman with stringy brown hair and a dark mole under her right eye. She was a real community organizer type on the scale of organizing neighborhood Easter egg hunts and such. She'd taken charge of the assembly-line junk mail operation we'd all been hired for for the day. I'd been hoping to squeeze five or six hours out of it, but Gloria's efficiency was going to cut it back to three, maybe four, tops.

"The envelopes?" Mabel shouted back. She was a woman past middle age, a divorcee, I guessed, or maybe a widow. "Over here by the little peel-off window-sticker thingees."

"I wonder if anybody ever puts those things on their windshield," Chris said, a guy in his thirties, like me, as if it were as ludicrous as smearing dogshit on the glass.

"I do," Gloria shot back, defiant, as if it were a question of loyalties. Technically, maybe, we were the company's employees for half a day, even if we *were* Prestos. But why Gloria's attitude?

I looked over at Chris, who rolled his eyes, a shared understanding. I shrugged my shoulders in sympathy.

After Gloria established the groups we set to work. Chris and I sealed the envelopes after Mabel and Shalita stuffed the stickers, the cover letters, the return envelopes and another couple of items that Gloria and

Jenny got out of the cardboard boxes and put into little piles. Gloria was a lean, fierce-looking Amazon wielding her boxcutter.

After we got into the rhythm, people started talking in pairs, conversationally.

"So," Chris said, "what do you do?"

I didn't know what he was getting at. What did I *do*? Like, for a living? It seemed pretty obvious.

"I don't know. What do *you* do?"

"I'm a writer, a poet."

"Oh yeah? So you sell books and stuff?"

"No, I write, when I find the time. And the inspiration."

I didn't know what to say to that so I didn't say anything.

"What do you do?" Chris asked me again.

"Well, this, I guess."

"Yes, but what do you *do*?"

"What do you mean, what do I *do*?"

"I mean, what do you *do*?"

I was still trying to formulate an answer when Gloria announced, "That's it. We're done."

I looked at the clock. Three and a half hours.

"So we're going to call it what, four hours?" I was all about the timesheet on this one. It'd been more than a week since I'd done an assignment and I knew my check was going to be pretty meager.

"More like three," Gloria said, but everybody grumbled a bit, and Shalita said "Bull*shit*."

"OK, it's four," Gloria said.

"Damn straight it's four," Shalita mumbled and I high-fived her.

The reality was we all needed the money and there wasn't any point in working for free. Plus, some of us had had to pay bus fare to get here, and just getting here took time. When did the clock start, anyway? Shouldn't we call it more like five hours? But I wasn't going to argue.

Chris read my thoughts and said, "Maybe we should call it five," but Gloria, the self-appointed supervisor, wouldn't have any of that, and nobody felt like arguing.

"I don't believe in gettin' nothin' handed to you," Mabel observed, as we all walked out into the sunshine. "If it ain't worth workin' for it ain't worth havin'." By her accent I guessed she was from West Virginia, and I remembered that song from Dylan's born again phase, "Slow Train Coming." *She was a backwoods girl but she sure was realistic.*

Extra

"Hello, Mom? Hey, I just thought you'd be interested to know I'm going to be in a movie."

I knew it would get her attention, but she was clued in to the irony that always drips from me like a leaky faucet. She was not about to do backflips or jumping jacks. Her congratulations were skeptical.

"Yes, it's through Presto," I admitted when she asked (accused?). "I'll be spending a couple of days as an extra in a synagogue scene. 'I am not Prince Hamlet, nor was meant to be. Am an attendant lord, one that will do to swell a progress, start a scene or two.'" Of course she recognized Eliot.

"No, I don't actually know what the movie's about, really, but I'll be playing a Jew on Yom Kippur.

"No! Of course you don't have to *be* Jewish! They didn't check to see if I was circumcised! I just wear a dark suit and a white skullcap and sit in the pews with a bunch of similarly clad men. It's an Orthodox synagogue and the women are up in the balcony.

"But wasn't Dad's grandmother Jewish? Or was it his grandfather?"

****

"Just take a seat in the pew there," one of the movie crew directed, a young guy with slicked hair and a clipboard. "Rabbi Konheim – he's the character Catanzaro's playing – is going to come down the aisle with the Torah – somebody else will actually be carrying the scrolls – shaking hands with the congregants. This scene will take all day; we'll have to shoot it several times. Just smile and nod, unless he offers his hand to shake, then shake it."

"Catanzaro?" the guy next to me said to the guy next to him. They were here together, it looked like. "Is he Jewish? The name doesn't sound Jewish."

"He *looks* Jewish, Avi," his friend replied. "Don't you think he looks Jewish?"

"Italians, Jews." Avi shrugged, and then he nudged me. "You think Catanzaro looks Jewish?"

I shrugged back. Sure, why not?

"Hey, mind if I switch seats with you? I'd kind of like to shake his hand, maybe make it into the movie." I had the seat right on the aisle.

"Sure, why not?" Sometimes it felt like my motto, like something Alfred E. Newman, the *MAD Magazine* guy, might say. *Sure, why not?*

"What about you?" Avi's friend said, as if he were coming to my defense. I wasn't sure if he was asking me if I were Jewish.

"Presto," I said.

"What?"

"I got this gig through a temp agency. Presto."

"Oh, I see. I just thought you might like to shake Catanzaro's hand when he comes by. Name's Ira," he said, sticking out his hand for a shake. "Avi and I are members here. We're doing this for free, had to sign a waiver to donate our wages to the Holocaust Museum in Washington. At least we get the free lunch. And the experience. Anybody know the name of the actress playing Catanzaro's wife?"

"Quiet, everybody!" the guy with the clipboard called. "Scene six, take one."

It was going to be a long day, and when Catanzaro came down the aisle he did not shake Avi's hand, or Ira's, or mine, for that matter. And when the movie came out a few months later, I wasn't able to recognize myself in the longshot of the sea of dark suits and white yarmulkes.

But my mom told me she saw the movie three times anyway.

Survey

"How highly would you rate terrorism as an issue of importance, on a scale from one to ten, ten being highly important?"

"Oh, Geez, I don't know. It's up there. But like, more people die in automobile accidents in a week than in terrorist attacks in a year."

"So..." – pencil hovering over the bubbles – "A two, maybe? Maybe a five?"

"Six. Let's give it a six."

I darken the bubble.

"But wait, fuck. Nine eleven. I mean, if there was another nine eleven."

"So, seven? Eight?"

"Oh, let's just leave it a six."

Another survey-taking job. It seemed like a billion-dollar industry at least. It was still a few years before the next census, when I'd be able to suck on the government tit for a few weeks, anyway, if not months, but somebody was always taking a poll about something or other, and they always needed people to ask the questions. Revenge of the temps. I actually enjoyed these little three-to-five-day gigs. You sort of learned things about your fellow human beings, though if pressed to say what, exactly, I'd be at a loss for words.

"On a scale from one to ten, how would you rate privacy issues as important, in the face of national security concerns?"

"Oh, where to begin? I don't know."

"I mean, is it important?"

"Oh Jesus. Five. Let's give it a five."

My assignment was to walk around the mall and ask random people. Age, race, sex and income questions up front, for the numbers-crunchers to sort out the random samples. I wandered around the food court and the wide-open space with the benches and skylight, stopping likely people, people who didn't look like they were in a hurry, just loitering, lounging.

"How would you rate the economy on a scale of one to ten?"

"Look, dude. I find this hard to quantify."

"Well, you know, is it very important, not important. You can put approximate numbers on it. One, two or three for not important, eight nine or ten for important. Just pick one."

"Let's come back to this one. What's next?"

"Reproductive rights, marriage equality, campaign finance reform."

"Are you a Republican or Democrat? I have to know who's asking these questions."

"I'm a Presto."

""You're Independent?"

"Like I said, I'm just a Presto."

The Perfect Storm

"It was the perfect storm," Marge was saying. "Two of their clerks already had vacation plans made. One was going on a cruise, the other had a family timeshare in a cottage on Lake Huron or someplace, and then another's mother suddenly died, and another quit, just when the students were going to start coming back for the fall semester and needed all that hand-holding."

"Why'd the clerk quit?" I didn't really care, but I thought I should say something. But then Marge didn't say anything for such a long pause, and I thought maybe the connection had been cut. "Marge? You still there?"

"I don't know. Who knows?" It was the kind of denial of knowledge that sounded like concealment but I let it pass.

"So about a week, you think?"

"It could even lead to something full time."

It was Marge's constant refrain. Did she get some kind of placement fee? A kickback, a percentage? Did she just assume this was what everybody wanted, a salary, benefits, health care coverage, vacation and sick time, a pension? A 401K?

"OK, I haven't got any plans, and it'll be air-conditioned, so I'm in. Dog Days of August be damned. When do I start?"

****

Susan Wallace, the office manager from hell. A sexy dark-haired girl in a loose summer dress and flip-flops, but for all the appearance of being "laid back," a real martinet.

"We're understaffed as I'm sure Marjorie told you, and it's new student week," Susan began, ignoring the hand I'd extended. "So you won't be getting a lunch break, I'm afraid, and you'll have to request a replacement at the desk for any bathroom breaks. And only one of those in the morning and one in the afternoon." I'd been assigned to a little desk at the entry to the Student Registration Building. Students would come in in a kind of panic and I'd take down their vitals, notify the secretaries to the counselors, who would meet further with the students and then assign the students times to meet with the counselors themselves. Many levels of bureaucracy at work. Then the students would come back to me so that I could tell them when the secretaries called me to tell them to meet with the counselors.

"Peter's pretty stressed right now," Susan confided. Susan ran this whole show, the temps, the secretaries, the counselors, the dean, and incidentally the students. Peter was Peter Graham, Dean of Something or Other. Chances are he was not the one who was "stressed."

"I'll take that book, too," she said, indicating the novel I had brought along with the superfluous sack lunch, Saul Bellow's *Dangling Man.* "No time for reading on this job. I thought you'd have known that already."

I could stick it out for a week, I figured, but I suddenly

understood Marge's mysterious reluctance to speak on the phone and kicked myself for not picking up on the signals about why the clerk had quit. The perfect storm, indeed.

Bartender

"Hello, I'm from the Presto temp agency. They sent me here to bartend a party?" I never know how to introduce myself without sounding like a fraud, as if the job might just be a practical joke on me, as if Marge had sent me chasing after a wild goose. Bartending at a New Year's Eve party at an Elks Club? Really?

"Come to the right place. Name's Gray, Dale Gray. I'm the manager. Just call me Dale."

I told him my name but he already had a nickname for me, Highpockets. Wasn't that some old-fashioned moniker for a tall person? I'm not even six feet. Maybe he just had a name he wanted to use. I've been called worse.

"Gene, Marilee, Jimbo, this is Highpockets. He's filling in tonight for Bruce. Bruce is sick, dammit. Called in this morning."

It was a busy night. I'd never actually bartended before, but I knew the basic recipes – highballs, Manhattans, Martinis, beer, shots – and what I didn't know I asked Gene, who was helpful, seemed to get a charge out of showing me the ropes. He was a fast-moving little bald guy who seemed to always be catching up with himself. "Behind you with the glasses!" he'd call, in case somebody made a move and bumped into him, breaking the freshly washed glasses.

Toward midnight, Pinkie, a drunk little middle-aged

woman who'd been sloshing Seven-and-Sevens all night long, started singing a song from her high school. "Shelbyville, Shelbyville, you are it! 'S-h' for 'Shelbyville' and 'i-t' for 'it.'" Then she'd laugh and chug her drink and start all over.

"Don't mind Pinkie," Gene whispered to me. "She's just feelin' her oats."

Pinkie's husband Ted was the Grand Wazir or whatever they called him, the head guy who donned the helmet with the antlers (I figured him for a cuckold anyway) and led the solemn pledge during the Hour of the Elk, at eleven PM, before the party wound down. Members were generally pretty cocky, treating the waitresses and bartenders like servants – the privileges of membership – but Pinkie seemed especially self-confident, uninhibited, and she sidled up to Dale Gray as if she were the lady of the plantation flirting with the overseer, like some Gothic scene out of Faulkner, building him up while putting him in his place.

"Shelbyville, Shelbyville, you are it," Pinkie began again, nuzzling into Gray's chest, the aroma of perfume and alcohol poofing out at all of us behind the bar.

The dance band that evening was called Cliff Gee and the Outlaws. They were pretty pathetic, botching songs halfway through, out of tune, unrehearsed. Several of the Elks complained, many rolled their eyes.

After midnight, an hour after the sacred oath, the new

year already getting older, the night coming to a close, Pinkie's fragrance still in his nose, her touch still on his chest, Dale Gray swaggered over to the band and ordered, "You guys get lost, why don't you? You're embarrassing."

Cliff, the shaggy mountain of a bandleader, insulted at being so summarily dismissed, humiliated in front of everybody, bellowed back, "I'm going to kick your ass way into February, Dale Gray, you little piece of shit." But he and the others packed up their instruments and equipment and headed for the door.

Cliff whirled around and pointed again at Dale. "I'm going to beat the living shit out of you, Gray!" he threatened.

"'S-h' for 'Shelbyville' and 'i-t' for 'it'!"

Gray came over to where the bartenders were breaking down the bar, capping bottles, washing the last glasses, wiping down the bar, putting away the condiments, sweeping the floor.

"You better be out there and ready to rumble if there's any trouble," Gray snarled. "That means you, too, Highpockets."

Of course, the parking lot was empty when we all turned off the lights and left the club, half an hour later, but it left me wondering where my duties as a Presto ended and where my loyalties lay. I'm a separate-peace kind of guy, and Gray could have treated Cliff a lot more graciously, I'd thought.

Primary

I'd have thought they'd get volunteers from their own congregation, but for some reason the church, which served as the polling place for its neighborhood, had hired Prestos to work as greeters, guides and dispensers of cookies and coffee to voters on primary election day in April. Well, why not? I was game. The gig was unclear, and the three of us kind of made it up as we went along, greeting voters, directing them to the booths where the election officials were to assist them in casting ballots (a sort of Rube Goldberg affair of three of four different lines, for getting ballots, for filling in the blanks on the paper ballots, for scanning them into the electronic readers), showing them where the bathrooms were, the handicapped exits, handing out the cookies and snacks, even offering to guide them around the sanctuary, not that I knew a nave from a vestibule, an altar from a tabernacle, let alone the particular history of this house of worship. Fortunately, I didn't have to conduct any tours. Temps often feel like interlopers, but I'd have felt like a downright fraud.

I'd already voted at my own polling place that morning – an elementary school where nobody had thought to offer cookies or coffee! – so I could politely decline the handouts, pamphlets, brochures and buttons offered by the gauntlet of campaign workers for the various candidates, outside the church when I showed up.

"Already voted! Just here to assist!" Virtue itself.

As my two co-workers and I handed out cookies and fielded questions, a small African-American boy came into the little chapel where we'd set up the goodies. He said his name was Jerome and he had the looks of a classic nerd – slender build, bug-eyed behind thick-framed glasses, buck teeth. The only thing missing was the violin case. His lower lip was quivering and his eyes behind the lenses brimmed with tears.

"I can't find my grandma anywhere," Jerome announced. He tried to keep his tone matter-of-fact but you could hear the quivering desperation under it, and, irrational as it was, I still felt the kid's sense of abandonment, vulnerability. I knew I had to talk him off the ledge of his feelings of desertion and loss.

"When did you last see her?"

"She out there handing out flyers for her candate," Jerome whimpered, mispronouncing the big word. "Her car's still there but I ain't seen her."

"Oh, her car's still here! Don't worry! She'll be back, Jerome! She probably just went to the bathroom or something. You stay right here and she'll be along, you'll see. Let's stay here and sing a little song," I suggested, sounding even to my own ears like one of those cheery adults you don't ever really trust. "Come on." I chose a toddler's song. I can't sing at all so my voice surely wouldn't intimidate him.

The ants go marching one by one, hurrah, hurrah.
The ants go marching one by one, hurrah, hurrah.
The ants go marching one by one.
The littlest ant was sucking his thumb.
The ants go marching, marching one by one.

"Now you try it, Jerome. Help me out here."

He looked at me, wary, refusing to participate but still wondering what the hell was going on here. So I continued.

The ants go marching two by two, hurrah, hurrah.
The ants go marching two by two, hurrah, hurrah.
The ants go marching two by two.
The littlest ant was sniffing glue.
The ants go marching, marching two by two.

This last verse got a little smile from him. I persevered.

The ants go marching three by three, hurrah, hurrah.
The ants go marching three by three, hurrah, hurrah.
The ants go marching three by three.
The littlest ant needed to pee.
The ants go marching, marching three by three.

At this point, Jerome was charmed by the silliness, and I could see the clown come out in him, always the nerd's defense against those who would bully him.

The ants go marching four by four, hurrah, hurrah.
The ants go marching four by four, hurrah, hurrah.

The ants go marching four by four.
The littlest ant walked through the door.
The ants go marching, marching four by four.

The ants go marching five by five, hurrah, hurrah.
The ants go marching five by five, hurrah, hurrah.
The ants go marching five by five.
The littlest ant was still alive.
The ants go marching, marching five by five.

We'd gotten up to the ants marching twenty-one by twenty-one when a voice from the entrance interrupted us.

"Jerome! Where you been?" We all turned to look at the older black woman, a red tee-shirt with her candidate's name in block white letters. "I been looking all over for you! I'm going back outside to pass out more flyers. Don't you go nowhere, hear?" Then she left and Jerome averted his eyes, blushing but no longer lost.

It was then that Linda, my Presto co-worker, said sternly, "Jerome, we found your grandma, and now we have work to do. We aren't just here to sing songs with you."

Getting the message, Jerome sheepishly got up out of his pew, gave me a little underhanded wave without looking at me, and scuttled out the door after his grandmother.

Dignity for Hire

I approached it as a job. Well, I stood to make as much as twenty grand for half an hour's work, so what more logical attitude to take? Friends had submitted my name. I hadn't really expected to be called, but here I was.

We all had to jump and wave our hands enthusiastically while the insipid theme song jingled out of overhead speakers like elephants on tiptoes. We shook our hips and hands, smiled as if we were trying to turn our mouths inside out.

Then the host, dressed like a lawyer at a high-profile trial – you know the guy I mean – came out from behind the curtain to studio audience applause and regarded us all with a kind of sardonic solemnity, as if he might break out laughing at any minute, roll around the floor. With the same straight face, he spoke to us as if we were a gathering of scholars, scientists at a symposium discussing cures for cancer, AIDS, Alzheimer's.

This guy could make eye contact without really looking at you. It was a real trick, the way he made you feel important and insignificant at the same time.

"For the win," he announced, like some sort of archangel proclaiming the end of time, "What does a woman do after her husband falls asleep?" The correct answer was based on a survey of a hundred random people interviewed at a Burger King in Arizona.

"Pig out on junk food?" Contestant A speculated.

"Do online shopping?" Contestant B ventured.

"Read a book?" I guessed, knowing it was the wrong answer.

None of us got the correct response, but we all walked away with a thousand dollars.

Twiddle her twanger? Really? Come on. I mean, really?

Go to Hell

For about ten years I was an adjunct in the English Department at a local community college. I showed up at night, after my day job as a technical writer, the campus deserted, the department offices empty. I liked it this way, the sense of being a kind of Zorro, no people in authority there to put me in my place. In fact, *I* was the authority figure.

I taught English 101, composition and rhetoric, one class each semester, always at night. The students wrote essays – narrative essays, descriptive essays, analytical essays, comparative essays, persuasive essays, a whole series of essays – and my job was to grade them. We read samples in the text book, discussed them, did writing exercises in class, when we weren't doing grammar lessons – it's and its, whose and who's, complete sentences, punctuation.

In my very first English 101 class, a dreamy-eyed kid named Jeremy slouched in a backrow seat. He wore a baseball cap with the slogan, "Go to Hell" on the visor. But he wasn't a troublemaker at all. Not that he was very engaged in class, but he wasn't disruptive, either. Once, in fact, I had to ask him not to light matches. He seemed to be lost in some sort of "experiment," oblivious to the rest of the classroom, to see how long he could hold the match before the flame burned his fingers, how long he could stand the pain. He did not put up an argument when I asked him to stop. I was sure this kid would be gone before the semester was over. School did not seem to be his thing.

In the very first essay – a descriptive essay, for which we read and discussed Eudora Welty's "The Corner Store" and Salman Rushdie's "The Taj Mahal"— Jeremy wrote about his grandfather drowning his grandmother in the bathtub on Christmas Eve. It had been a mercy killing – the lady had Alzheimer's. Jeremy wrote about his head nearly exploding as he ran from the house, after the discovery, and walked the winter streets alone. The whole family had lived together.

Wow. This was basically what I found so fascinating about this job. The pay was pathetic. Fortunately, I did not have to try to make a living from my teacher's pay. It was like extra money for me, spending money, on top of the salary I got from my full-time job as a technical writer for an appliance manufacturer, writing instructions for using microwave ovens, assembling stand-up fans, and troubleshooting faulty toaster ovens. This was like real life. This was why I felt like Zorro.

Sure enough, after about five weeks, Jeremy stopped showing up in class. The rest of the class continued taking quizzes on misplaced and dangling modifiers, pronoun references and sentence fragments. They wrote a ten-page term paper complete with footnotes. They fretted about grades, but I was pretty generous on that score. Life was too short and difficult as it was. Why add to their troubles?

Milly Spaay, the Department chair, called me into her office after I'd turned in my grades one semester, about five or six years after I'd started teaching there.

"You're not doing them any favors by inflating their grades, Roger," she scolded.

But yeah, that's exactly what I was doing them – a favor. Go to hell, Milly.

How Sam Spade Got Me Hired and then Fired

I'd just graduated from college and wasn't sure what I wanted to do next – what sort of career I might pursue. While I sorted through my options – essentially different graduate school programs; I didn't have much ambition – I read Dashiell Hammett novels, no longer burdened with homework reading assignments. *The Maltese Falcon, Red Harvest, The Dain Curse.* I was especially captivated by the Continental Op, the nameless private investigator for the Continental Detective Agency in San Francisco, and I thought maybe that's what I'd do, become a private detective.

So naturally I started with the classified ads in *The Boston Globe.* I was living in a studio in Kenmore Square at the time, next to the Charles River. That was how I became a security guard for an outfit called Guardsmark, first step into the world of crime and detection. In my gray trousers with the blue stripe down the side, ersatz policeman's hat with the Guardsmark emblem on the bill, the shiny hard plastic visor, the badge straight from a cereal box, I looked like a guy going to a costume party. The employees at the places where I had my assignments – university buildings, warehouses, hospitals – all seemed to regard me as vaguely ridiculous, pathetic. I didn't care. I had my Raymond Chandler novels – having read all of Hammett – and all night to read, while I made my rounds with the watchclock key.

Unfortunately, the job got to be very boring very fast. After bouncing around the area, from Revere to Quincy, I'd settled into a long assignment at a hospital on Summit Avenue in Brookline, the smell of disinfectant pervasive and discouraging. I thought long and hard about taking the GREs and applying to graduate school. Philosophy? Literature? History? In the meantime, I was still reading the ads and my eye was caught by a weeklong program at a Professional Bartending School on Boylston Street. It sounded like it might provide more of the excitement I'd envisioned as a detective. Quotations from Hammett started coming to me. From *Red Harvest: This damned burg's getting me. If I don't get away soon I'll be going blood-simple like the natives.*

And then I thought, why not try my hand at some hardboiled prose? I had my boring nightly reports to fill out – time in, time out, *all quiet* – and who was reading these anyway? *Anybody?* At first it was just small descriptive stuff – *It was about eleven o'clock in the evening, mid-October, a bright moon behind a veil of clouds in the eastern sky...*

But soon I'd added suspense. *I was sure I'd heard a noise behind the cafeteria door and cautiously made my way in. The room was quiet, so deathly quiet it made me nervous. The sound of my heels on the linoleum was like gunshots.* I couldn't actually make up any incidents, so the prose itself had to do. The "atmosphere." *I'd never seen a community so gripped in fear.*

Unfortunately, the hospital administration was not amused. *That's* who was reading the reports! When I arrived at work one night, one of the Guardsmark supervisors was there to meet me. It was the 1970's, in the age before the internet, and I didn't have a telephone in my Kenmore Square studio apartment. This was the only way they could get in touch. Fortunately, Nick Asaro, my supervisor, whom I'd known since my Presto days, had a sense of humor, and as I'd already handed in my two-week notice – I was going to go to bartending school and take the GRE! – he let me go on my resignation letter, instead of terminating me. How would *that* have looked to a prospective employer, after all, that I'd been fired as a security guard for creative writing?

Stuck

"Long way to Quincy from Kenmore Square," Riley, the warehouse manager said when I reported for duty as the weekend security guard, duded up in my uniform: navy pants, officer's cap, badge and jacket. My first day. He had one of those squeaky Boston accents (*kwin-zee, ken-moah skuay-uh*).

"Green line to red line on the T, but yeah, took maybe an hour to get here," I nodded.

Riley looked me up and down, a guy in his fifties with a too-small herringbone sports jacket, a grease-spotted tie on a shirt that didn't button at the neck, a cigar in his hand like an extra finger.

It was 1975. I was taking a "gap year" between college and grad school, though it wasn't called that at the time. I'd come to Boston from Potawatomi Rapids, Michigan, where I'd gone to college, a Midwesterner through and through.

"You go see the Red Sawx much?" he asked around his cigar.

"Once or twice."

"Okay, well, this job ain't much. About the worst is some kids throwing stones at the warehouse (*wayuhhouse*) out back, but mostly it's slow around here (*aroun he-yuh*)."

"My commanding officer," I said, not sure what the

proper title was for my boss, Nick Asaro, "told me I should make the watchclock rounds every two hours, write up a report."

Riley flinched at that "commanding officer." He looked like he was probably a war vet, Korea or World War Two, and probably thought I was playing army or something. Commanding officer. What *should* I call him? I didn't even have a gun, not even a nightstick.

"Okay, I'll show you the rounds."

We walked through the various stations, covering enough of the building to get a thorough overview of the territory. If anything was amiss, I'd be sure to notice when I made my rounds.

"This elevator (*elevaytuh*) can get stuck sometimes," Riley said, puffing on his cigar, when we got to the back of the warehouse. He'd shown me all of the stations I needed to pass, the big clocks with the keyholes where I'd twist the key on my belt to show I'd been by.

I nodded.

"Just be careful." (*kehfil*)

I nodded.

"There," he pointed with his cigar out the back bay where the trucks drove up, "they're out there." (*They-uh they-uh out they-uh*). A group of teenagers roved around like feral cats, throwing railroad-sized rocks in the direction of the warehouse. He shook his head. "Kids," he muttered. Then he raised his voice, pointing the cigar between middle and pointer finger. "Get lost!" he shouted. They ignored him and we continued on our way, Riley unperturbed.

The service elevator was indeed unreliable. You pushed the buttons and it juddered up from the first to the second floor, protesting all the way. It was during my 4:00 AM rounds, a Styrofoam cup of burnt coffee in my hand, that the damn thing gave out between floors. Just stopped.

I began to panic when it wouldn't move, seeing myself stuck here until Monday morning when somebody showed up for work. I was stuck. In fact, I was stuck in my life, it occurred to me. What was I even doing here, working as a security guard? Had I thought it would be a cool, exciting gig, like Dashiell Hammett's Continental Op, instead of a tedious drudge? And what about graduate school next year? Did I really want to pursue a degree in Economics? Wouldn't a degree in Film Studies be more interesting? But my parents called that a waste of time.

And my romantic life? I was stuck there, too, going nowhere. I'd recently broken up with my girlfriend in Potawatomi Rapids, or rather, the relationship had died on its own. Shirley wanted to settle down in Muncie, Indiana, where her family lived, and she wanted me to settle down there with her, stuck in some sort of assistant manager job in a bank or some such. She'd spelled it out more than once. But I remembered being naked with her and my breath quickened with the memory of her body.

I'd just about given up trying to get the fucking elevator to work. For a couple of hours now I'd been pushing that unresponsive button like a B.F. Skinner pigeon pecking for food. But what else was there to do? Plus, the rancid coffee had worked its way through my system and I really needed to pee. I pressed the button again, and – *mirabile dictu* – the elevator started to move! Relief flooded over me when the doors opened on the second floor and I stepped out of the elevator.

Suddenly the idea of studying Economics seemed like a welcome, exciting prospect after all. Markets, fiscal policy, economic growth. And Shirley? Well, maybe getting back together with Shirley really wasn't such a good idea.

Taxi Driver

It was a year before the movie with Robert De Niro and Jodie Foster came out, but I still thought it would be a romantic adventure, more than just a job. Trouble was, I'd just moved to Boston from a tiny town in the Middle-west – Potawatomi Rapids, Michigan – that didn't even have one-way streets or left-turn arrows. But I figured the fares I picked up would know how to get to where they needed to be, right? How hard could it be?

I got a Hackney License downtown somewhere in Copley Square, no problem. I didn't have a criminal record, I'd just gotten a Massachusetts driver's license, I was over 21 (22 to be exact), a clean-cut corn-fed college kid.

I must have *looked* honest. The management at the taxi company over near Fenway Park hired me with no problems. My first day of work was the day the clocks jumped ahead an hour, February 23, a bleak, sleety, slushy morning. For some reason – one of the original "energy crises" – somebody had decided that starting daylight savings time in February was going to save power. I trudged over to get my cab from my rooming-house in Kenmore Square, a huge sprawling Romanesque Revival style building with conical towers built in 1901, the hallways of which were as confusing as a rabbits' warren.

My first – and only – fare I forgot to throw the meter. Fortunately, the guy was only going a short way, and he kindly gave me a five-dollar bill.

"You wanna go back to the garage," he confided, "hang a left onto Beacon."

I was way out of my depth, for sure. Reality had run smack into the crazy romantic dream of a madcap escapade. I headed back through Kenmore Square, a middle-aged lady on Commonwealth Avenue yoohooing at me with her scarf. I ignored her, driving on and turning into Brookline Avenue and on toward Landsdowne Street, back to the taxi company, like the Trojans fleeing inside the walled city, escaping the Greeks. Smartest thing I ever did in my life, even if I felt like a failure, my pride a dirty doormat.

Inside the garage, I got out of my cab, handed the dispatcher my keys and the five-dollar bill, explaining my folly to him, pleading incompetence. No harm, no foul. He agreed I should maybe try again some other time when I was more familiar with the area. I could have sworn he was the same guy I'd once had an altercation with as a pretzel-bike vendor outside the art museum a few years back. Then I went back to the Charlesgate and crawled into bed. When I woke up a few hours later, I began scheming about Plan B.

The Same River Twice

> "...people as confident as Roxanne often seemed
> to get the better of me, even if it was only by
> not listening."
>   – "Some Women" by Alice Munro

I thought Jackie was dumb as rocks, if you want to know the truth, but the teachers all liked her because she volunteered to decorate the gym for high school dances, and they gave her B's that probably should have been C's or D's, but that never stopped her from talking down to me, as if I didn't understand. Mainly it was her looks that gave her the confidence, and being an extrovert on the cheerleading squad. She was a wiry little blond girl, not ugly but not a knock-out either, but she thought of herself as good-looking, a catch. Her long hair spread down to her shoulders like a cowl and was always neatly combed, if dry as the straw in an Easter egg basket.

So anyway, all these years later I ran into Jackie at my 50th high school reunion. Hadn't really thought of her in years, though there was a brief time at the beginning of the century when e-mail groups flourished, and there was a Potawatomi Rapids Class of 1967 group that I joined from the same sense of curiosity everybody else did, only to realize there was a reason we *hadn't* stayed in touch – just no chemistry. The email group petered out within a year.

Speaking of Chemistry, that's what I do; it's my field. I teach at Algonkian College in Virginia. In fact, I've met Eric Betzig as a colleague. He was at the Howard Hughes Medical Institute in Ashburn at the time, may still be. He won the 2014 Nobel Prize in Chemistry, with two other scientists, for their work in single-molecule microscopy. I even attended a lecture by Bill Moerner, from Stanford, one of the other two co-winners.

I'm not a name-dropper, but I thought it was pretty cool and I mentioned it to Billy Shuster, another of my class-mates, now a retired pharmacist. I saw Jackie out of the corner of my eye making sarcastic little baby movements with her mouth to Sherry Morris – *nyaa-nyaa-nyaa* – and rolling her eyes at me as if I were some sort of snob. What had I done to offend her? Did she think I was boasting? Or was it Billy Shuster she was mocking?

"Jackie!" I sang out. "Jackie McNulty!" I used her maiden name.

She turned to me then as if only noticing me for the first time, and she blushed at Sherry, and I knew it was me she'd been scorning. If she had a job, this was its description, "mean girl."

"Justin! So good to see you back home!" Jackie hadn't left Potawatomi Rapids. Her husband, Blake Rodgers, had died fifteen years before. Blake had taken over his father's plumbing business and now their son Randy ran it. She made me remember my college girlfriend, Shirley, her fantasies about our life together in Muncie, Indiana.

"I'd ask you to dance," Jackie smiled, "but I remember you never did go out on the floor with the rest of us."

And just like that she put me in my place.

Mother's Little Helper

What a drag it is getting old...

How old were the Stones when they wrote that, Geldon wondered, listening to the song on the car radio as he headed home from the gym. Twenty-two? Twenty-three? True, it was supposed to be in the voice of an anonymous, depressed middle-aged housewife, but still... Mick Jagger had just turned seventy-two a few weeks earlier, he reflected.

Geldon had retired a year before from the State Revenue Department, but here he was about to enter the workforce again, all because he'd panicked three months after retiring and inquired about teaching a class at Downtown University. The program director, Mona Terry, had been encouraging but warned that there probably wouldn't be an opening until the next fall. Still, Geldon, who had taught composition and rhetoric as a part-time instructor at one of those for-profit outfits whose television commercials typically featured beaming, inarticulate kids and middle-aged men and women re-tooling for second careers in information technology and refrigerator repair, went about submitting a resume, getting references, completing online forms.

Now, over a year into retirement, he'd received an e-mail from Mona asking him if he were still interested. What could he say? Yes, he wrote back, he was still interested. Mona sent him a 50-page course outline for

Downtown University's composition classes, and said she would be back in touch when the schedule became a bit clearer.

Geldon remembered his mother back in Potawatomi Rapids, Michigan. She'd worked until the day she died, practically, cleaning other people's houses. In her mid-seventies, cleaning old Mrs. Ahmogamp's home, fixing her breakfast and doing her laundry, Mrs. Geldon had acted as if she'd had her whole life ahead of her, and then *bam!* pancreatic cancer, and she was dead after a brief but agonizing illness.

When Geldon had left Potawatomi Rapids for college and a life in the city all those years ago, he'd vowed never to return. But wasn't he just repeating his mother's mistakes? Mother's little helper indeed.

After two weeks, when he hadn't heard from Mona, the new semester looming – Geldon had already had a nightmare about going to the first class without a syllabus prepared – he wrote to her and asked if the schedule was any clearer now.

Mona! It seemed like such an old-fashioned name, a name that would never be a top-ten baby-girl name, a girl-next-door name. It had a primordial ring to it for Geldon, from deep down in the Mississippi Delta, or from the far-flung Appalachian hills and hollows, the bleak western deserts. The moan in the name was both erotic and threatening, savage and sublime. For some reason it made him think of Marge, that long-ago supervisor from his Presto days.

And now, from the *ping!* on his iPhone as he'd driven away from the gym, he saw she'd responded. Yes no yes no yes no. What kind of class did she have to offer him? Daytime? Night? Once a week? Three times? Could he ask for a sample syllabus this late in the game? What about the pacing of assignments? He'd read about the "portfolio" the students were to submit at the end of the semester, with assignments sheets, original drafts, revisions. Geldon groaned inwardly. *Fuck! Hadn't he escaped this bullshit a year ago?*

When Geldon got home, he tossed the soiled gym clothes into the hamper, poured himself a cup of re-heated coffee, fired up the computer and prepared to meet his fate.

Dear Mister Geldon:

Thank you very much for following up with me about this. I am emailing to let you know that we have just completed our fall staffing, and we have no need of additional instructors, after all.
I sincerely appreciate your interest in our program, and I'll be happy to keep your application materials on file in case openings arise in future semesters.

Thanks again,
Mona Terry

Oh, thank you, thank you, thank you, Mona! Geldon thought, relieved. He felt he'd dodged a bullet. Keep my application materials as long as you want! He took a triumphant sip of his re-heated coffee, only to feel the soot of coffee grounds on his tongue.

What a drag it is getting old.

Acknowledgments

"Bartender," "Hell Is Other People," "Information Technology," "Dignity for Hire," "How Sam Spade Got Me Hired and then Fired," "Stuck," "Taxi Driver," "The Same River Twice," and "Mother's Little Helper" in *Work Literary Magazine*

"Survey" in *Sonic Boom*

"Turf War," "Duplicity" and "Reality" in *Meat for Tea*

"Extra" in *No Extra Words*

"The Perfect Storm" in *Brilliant Flash Fiction*

"Go to Hell" in *The Zodiac Review*

BAMBOO
DART
PRESS

112 N. Harvard Ave. #65
Claremont, CA 91711

chapbooks@bamboodartpress.com

www.bamboodartpress.com